This Walker book
belongs to:

_____

_____

_____

Should someone
cast a spell on me,
come, best friend,
and set me free.

For
Sarah, Jim and Zachary

First published 2009 by Walker Books Ltd
87 Vauxhall Walk, London SE11 5HJ

This edition published 2010

4 6 8 10 9 7 5 3

© 2009 Penny Dale

The right of Penny Dale to be identified as author/illustrator of this work has been
asserted by her in accordance with the Copyright, Designs and Patents Act 1988

This book has been typeset in Goudy Hundred

Printed in China

British Library Cataloguing in Publication Data:
a catalogue record for this book is available from the British Library

ISBN 978-1-4063-2429-7

www.walker.co.uk

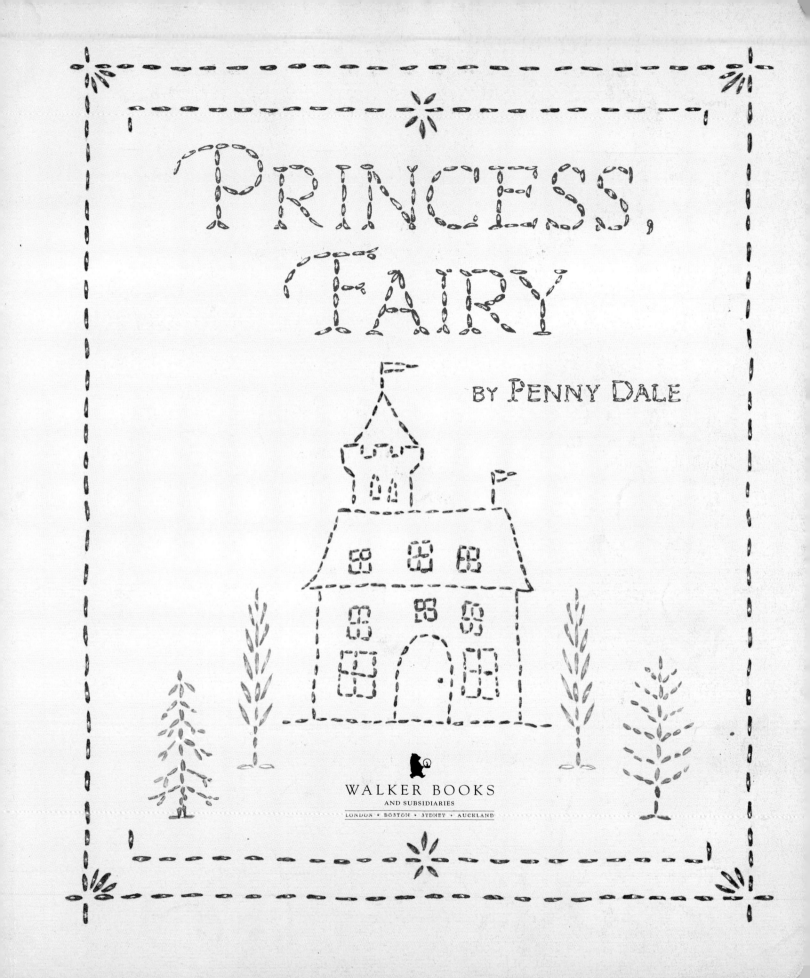

PRINCESS, FAIRY

BY PENNY DALE

WALKER BOOKS
AND SUBSIDIARIES
LONDON · BOSTON · SYDNEY · AUCKLAND

A princess in a magic garden
was playing with
her golden ball ...

when, *splash!*
her ball fell in the water and sank
deep, deep down, out of sight.

Then a little frog appeared.
"Princess, promise me a kiss
and I will find your ball,"
it croaked.

"I promise," she replied.

And so the frog dived down,
deep down,
and there it found the golden ball ...

and brought it back.
"Now kiss me as you promised.
Kiss me!"
croaked the frog.

But the princess turned away.
"I can't kiss you; you're just a frog.
A horrid little frog!" she said.

And home she went to her palace.
But deep, deep down,
the princess knew
she should not have
broken her promise.

If only she could make things right.
Just then came a *knock! knock! knock!*
at the door.

It was the frog!
"Please will you kiss me,
princess," it croaked.

"Yes," said the princess, "I will!"

So the princess knelt
and kissed the frog
and magic happened!

A spell was broken
and the frog became ...

a fairy!

Princess, Fairy – here our story ends –
playing in the magic garden,
happy ever after, best friends!

Happy am I
for knowing this –
there's magic in
a best friend's kiss.

Other books
by Penny Dale: